'Twas the First Night Before Christmas

Mary Beth Vonk

ISBN: 0615856071
ISBN-13: 9780615856070
Library of Congress Control Number: 2013913879
Mary Beth Vonk, Norfolk, NE

'Twas the night before Christmas
when all through the town
Not a creature was stirring
or making a sound.

Joseph and Mary arrived
in Bethlehem's square
In hopes to find lodging
and birth Jesus there.

The people were nestled
all snug in their beds.
"No more rooms in the inn,"
the innkeeper said.

Poor Mary, great with Child,
was eager to nap.
The innkeeper led them
to a stable out back.

Nearby, in a field,
there arose such a clatter.
Shepherds sprang from their beds
to see what was the matter.

Way up in the night sky
appeared a great flash
Revealing an angel
with a bright golden sash.

The light from the angel
produced a strong glow
Giving luster of midday
to objects below.

When what to their wondering
eyes did appear?
But a sky full of angels
bringing joyous, good cheer.

They said, "Go to the city
of David real quick
To see Yahweh's Savior,
His number one pick."

More rapid than hiccups
the birth pangs they came.
Mary brought forth a son
and she called him by name,

"Oh Jesus, Messiah,
Creator, and King,
Immanuel, Day Star,
Jehovah's Offspring."

He will hang on a cross
beyond Jerusalem's wall.
Ransomed captives released.
He'll atone for us all.

The shepherds made haste
almost seeming to fly.
Found Mary and told her
'bout the angel-filled sky.

Her baby was God in the Flesh.
She just knew.
With a heart full of love,
she pondered this, too.

Joseph held baby Jesus
beneath stable's roof.
They heard prancing and pawing
of animal hooves.

The very next day,
Joseph searched all around.
He returned with a smile
for the house that he found.

Baby Jesus was swaddled
from his head to his foot,
And they whisked Him away
to a home that was good.

Wise men saw a new star
and searched through scrolls way back.
Israel's Savior was born!
They started to pack.

Gold, frankincense, myrrh
for the babe to make merry
Were gifts from the East
that the camels did carry.

They traveled in caravan
with many in tow
And rejoiced in the eve'
when they saw the star's glow.

Israel's king asked the wise men
'bout the scroll's prophecy.
"A new king replace me?"
Herod started to seethe.

Herod sent the wise men
to Bethlehem to see
And bring back the news
of the new king-to-be.

In the city of David,
they looked up above.
The star shone straight down
on the house full of love.

To Mary and Joseph
they said, "Do not dread.
We came to see Jesus
and kiss his sweet head."

They spoke no more words
but went straight to their work
And unloaded their gifts,
then turned with a jerk.

Being warned in a dream,
the wise men did know.
Don't return to King Herod
for he was a foe.

They sprang to their camels
to their team gave a whistle.
The wise men took off
like the down of a thistle.

Happy wise men were they
as they drove out of sight –
Proclaimed they to all,
"We have seen The Great Light!"

"For God so loved the world
that he gave his one and only Son,
that whoever believes in him
shall not perish but have eternal life.
For God did not send his Son
into the world to condemn the world,
but to save the world
through him."

(JOHN 3:16-17)

Merry Christmas!

Made in the USA
Monee, IL
17 December 2021

86160856R00017